Return To Dog Island

Copyright © 2007 Aaron A. Lehman
All rights reserved.
ISBN: 1-4196-7445-5
ISBN-13: 978-1419674457

Library of Congress Control Number: 2007905695

Visit www.booksurge.com to order additional copies.

AARON A. LEHMAN

RETURN TO DOG ISLAND

2007

Return To Dog Island

To Carson, Anita and Keith

ACKNOWLEDGEMENTS:

Pauline Auger- Aboriginal Education Teacher

Keith Denoncourt- "Essential Guide to Wilderness Survival", Outdoor Education Teacher

Helen Gall- Sketches

Kelly Harlton- Wildside Wilderness Connection

MJ Munn-Kristoff- Forest Education

Ron Lambert- Sled Dog Training

Trudie Moon- Computer

Terry Mosher- Editing

OTHER SOURCES:

Recreating the Birch Bark Canoe- Mike Camp

The Fur Trade at Lesser Slave Lake - William Peter Baergen

Archaeological Research in the Lesser Slave Region - Raymond J. Le Blanc

A History Of Lesser Slave Lake - Geoff Sawyer

The Bark Canoes and Skin Boats of North America - U.S. National Museum Bulletin 230

CHAPTER 1

"Pole! Pole hard!!!" Raymond screamed to the old Indian man, with gray braided hair, who was wearing a tattered, moose hide coat.

Hunched over, the man strained on a long pole to push himself over the frothing whitecaps on Lesser Slave Lake. The lake boiled as a strong, west wind swept across the expanse of open water between the lake shore and Dog Island.

"Pole! Pole hard!!!"

From a distance, Raymond could see a small party of warriors gaining on the old man. Spears were raised and he could hear the war cries echoing across the water. The warriors were paddling sleek, slender, birch bark canoes with their arching bows and sterns, slicing the water, rising and falling in rhythm with the rolling waves. The powerful strokes of the warriors easily guided the canoes through the whitecaps and propelled them toward the struggling, old Indian.

"Look behind!!" Raymond yelled again.

Raymond couldn't believe what he was seeing! The Indian was poling a somewhat round water craft which looked like half of a big balloon floating in the water. A rough frame of willow branches gave the balloon some shape and it looked as if a moose hide or some kind of animal skin was stretched over it to make a crude skin boat. The long pole touched the bottom of the lake and the old man struggled to push forward against the strong wind, the waves and the swirling of the skin boat. Controlling the boat was difficult because there was no front or back and the current took it in many directions, sometimes spinning it in the wind.

"Paddle! Paddle hard!!"

The pole no longer reached the bottom of the lake. The old man still tried to paddle himself forward with the pole, but it was too narrow to make a difference. Spinning, splashing through the whitecaps, taking on water, this craft was doomed as the warriors swept in for the kill with their superior canoes. Spears slashed through the fragile skin. Water gushed in. The boat filled with water and the old man started to sink. A few desperate attempts to stay afloat, combined with some flailing and thrashing were not enough to save the old man and he disappeared under the water as the warriors cheered.

War cries!!

They are coming for me in my skin boat!!
Pole! Pole hard!!

A strong warrior himself, Raymond would meet the foreign warriors head on.

"You killed my mosôm! I'll teach you to pick on an old man!"

Raymond tried to steer his own skin boat, but it just spun and went in every direction as the waves of the storm pounded it. He poled with his strong arm muscles bulging, but the waves overpowered him. The warriors were closing in, with their streamlined canoes.

Help!! No bottom!

The pole floated loose in Raymond's hand.

No more poling. Paddle!! Paddle hard!!

With no bottom to push on, Raymond had no control of his skin boat. The waves washed over the flapping skin, the wind spun the flimsy craft around and as hard as he paddled the pole, he was doomed. The warriors pounced on him from their sleek, birch bark canoes and they slashed large holes in his boat with their sharp, flint spears.

Help!! Help!!

Water swept over Raymond as the boat filled with water and the whitecaps pounded his body as he went under the surface. His strong arms allowed him to swim for a short distance, but the warriors watched as he went down for the last time.

CHAPTER 2

"Help!! Help!!" Raymond yelled.
"Wake up you crazy Indian!" Larry yelled back.
Larry was Raymond's white stepbrother, who was sleeping in the single bed on the other side of the small, upstairs room. Banners of hockey teams and racing snowmobiles covered the cracked walls and ceiling. Raymond's parents were not rich, but they provided a comfortable and safe home for their three children.

"What is your problem?" Larry asked.

"I guess I had a dream and I thought I was drowning," Raymond responded, still half thinking he was under water. Tears came to his eyes as he thought about his grandpa being attacked by the warriors and drowning.

Why were we being attacked? Will I drown in the lake sometime? Did my môsom drown in the lake? I was told that Môsom went missing in a blizzard on Dog Island. Maybe that was just a story to cover up what really happened. Why isn't there any sign of him? I tried to look on Dog Island last winter with my snowmobile, but a crash ended that.

"Time to get up! School day!" Rose called. Rose was Raymond's Cree mother and she tried to get her kids to school on time.

Why does she always have to act like a white woman? She is Cree and she should be letting me grow up Cree. If I were up North with my father, I'd be out trapping, and fishing. No school. I hate school!

Raymond didn't want to go to school today. He didn't have his math homework done. *Aarrgh!* Then he remembered. They were going to start building a birch bark canoe for Careers and Technology Studies class. Two Cree elders, Mabel and Sam, had agreed to show the class how to build a canoe as the aboriginal people had done long ago.

"I'm coming."

"I beat you!" Emily called from the bathroom.

"Rats."

Emily, Raymond's half sister, had the other bedroom upstairs, on the closer side of the rickety, squeaky stairway. Emily needed lots of time to fix her hair just right. She always tried to beat the boys.

Now, we'll have to wait forever! Emily doesn't have any trouble fitting in as a white girl. She doesn't look Indian like I do. I hate being Indian! Yet, a minute ago, I wanted to live up North as an Indian! I'm so mixed up!

Raymond did his usual exercises as he waited, push-ups and sit-ups mixed with other stretches he had learned in Phys. Ed. His muscles were showing nicely and he was gaining strength, in general. He needed lots of muscles to show off his six foot frame.

Wow! I look dark! Raymond thought when he finally got to look in the bathroom mirror. *Maybe it's just that Larry and Allen are so much white!*

Allen was Raymond's step-dad and Larry was Allen's son. They were both very blond. Raymond had a dark, aboriginal coloured skin, long black hair and dark eyes.

If I went to a city school, I would be light compared to some of those guys. On the other hand, maybe I should make a braid and look like a real Indian.

How about this? Raymond smiled as he used one of Emily's elastic bands to make a pony tail.

Why not?

"Raymond. We're going to be late!"

Mother again! "I'm coming." *Why is she always harping on me?*

Rose dropped the kids off at school on her way to work. Raymond often walked to school, but he was late this morning and he had to get his math homework done before the first bell.

Too late! The bell's gone. Maybe I can get it done in English class.

Raymond slammed the scratched, dusty gray locker door and he clicked the lock shut. He had to jostle his way through a mass of other kids running and scuffling off to classes.

I hate it here. If I were up North I could be alone and take care of myself. I wouldn't have to fight through a crowd. I could go wherever I wanted to with my snowmobile.

Then, Raymond remembered that he had crashed his snowmobile.

"Okay," Mr. Johnson said as Raymond slunk into his seat.

"Today, I want you to write a story about something that has happened to you this week. Use good language skills and make it interesting."

No luck in doing Math! Now, I have to write a story! Yuk! No one wants to hear about my boring life. Nothing interesting happens to me. Hey, wait a minute! How about a wild dream? Everyone will laugh at it and make Indian jokes. However, maybe I can squeeze in the Math if I hurry.

"Hey, Raymond," Jack whispered. "What's with the pony tail? You trying to be a real Indian?"

"Yeah. You jealous?"

Jack was Raymond's white friend and he liked to tease. Raymond liked to tease as well, but the Indian jokes did hurt in a way. By teasing and joking, Raymond could get along better with his classmates. Raymond didn't have a lot of friends, but he didn't have any enemies either. He and Jack weren't party animals, but they had a lot of fun together, especially on the weekends. They both liked the out-of-doors, snowmobiling, swimming in the lake and skiing. Jack was a good hockey player on a local team. Raymond didn't play on a team, but he liked to play street hockey with friends and he joined Jack for a friendly game on ice once in a while. Sometimes, he went to watch Jack play at the local ice arena.

"Okay, Raymond," Mr. Johnson said, "let's hear your story."

Scared, Raymond started to read the story about his dream. His legs were shaking and a bead of sweat was gathering on his upper lip. Quivers appeared in his voice and he never raised his head to look at the other kids. Raymond hated talking in front of the class. He preferred to be the silent Indian, as his classmates called him.

When he had finished, he slipped into his seat, wishing he could disappear. To his amazement, everyone clapped and cheered.

"Interesting story," Mr. Johnson said, "but, you were supposed to tell about a real experience."

Raymond figured his dream was real enough, but that would have to wait, for he was off to his next class.

I did it! I told about my Indian dream, and they liked it.

Math went okay, but he wondered who would ever use geometry?

I'll probably flunk this course if I keep missing my homework. Why learn a bunch of theorems I'll never use? I'd rather be up North, hunting and trapping!

After lunch, the CTS class boarded a bus and they headed to a Black Spruce bog. They didn't have to go far because many bogs and marshes, mixed with the large trees of the Boreal forest, were located close to Slave Lake. In fact, many of the oil and gas fields, so important to the local economy, were found under bogs. The class needed to find materials for a birch bark canoe. Of course, they needed birch bark, but also Black Spruce roots for sewing the bark together and spruce pitch for sealing the seams. Mabel and Sam knew of a good place.

It will be great to get out in the bush, but I'd rather be working on an engine or fixing my snowmobile. They'll probably do that Indian culture stuff again. They figure I should know all about that, but I don't. Mother doesn't say anything about her culture and Marg doesn't talk much, unless I ask her about the old ways.

After the bus stopped, they had to jump across a ditch and push through a dense tangle of willow shrubs to follow a narrow game trail. Once they were through the brush, a damp, swampy smell greeted them. It was a dark landscape, shrouded in hues of dark green and black, with grayish, stringy stuff hanging from many of the brittle branches of the stunted trees. It looked like a Halloween haunted house.

"Over here!" Mabel called. "What do you know about a bog?"

"Muskeg!" someone shouted.

"Yes," Mabel said. "The local name for all wet lands is muskeg. Actually, there are different types of muskeg."

"My dad lost a cat in the muskeg last year," Frank said.

"Did it have nine lives?" Hilda asked.

Everyone laughed. Hilda, an exchange student, didn't know about local happenings. In fact, three students in the class were from countries other than Canada. They took this class to learn more about Canadian aboriginal culture. Raymond couldn't figure out why they wanted to know about that. Most of the Indians he knew were trying to forget it.

"A cat is also a large tracked machine that clears land for forestry and oil field work," Sam said. "If they don't wait until the frost goes deep enough into the ground before driving on it, the heavy machine may sink."

"Actually," Mabel continued, "a bog is a mat of roots and moss that has grown over a shallow lake. Sometimes, there is still water underneath the mat, but most times it is just a thick layer of partially rotten vegetation."

"Jump up and down," Sam urged.

They all jumped up and down and the whole forest floor gave way and bounced as they jumped. It was fun.

"Pull back some of the moss," Mabel instructed.

The cool, moist, feather-like moss was soft and pleasant to touch. Underneath the olive green, living tops of the moss plants, they found a mass of brown, dead moss and a tangle of roots. Sometimes, the moss was covering an old, dead tree stump.

"It takes a long time for things to rot in the bog because it is soaked with cold water and the soil is acidic. North of Slave Lake, some of the wetlands are frozen all year round. This is called permafrost"

"What is this greenish wood I found?" someone asked as he pulled a blue-green chunk of wood from a rotten log.

"It is called Devil's wood," Sam said, "because it glows in the dark."

"Listen up!" Mabel called. "I want you to find me samples of four kinds of plants that are growing in the bog. Don't go too far and stay away from the water holes."

It wasn't too hard to find the different plants and the kids soon gathered around Mabel and Sam with their samples.

"How are these plants all alike?" Sam asked. "How are they different?"

Mabel identified the different plants. She held up samples of the plants common to the bog. These included Black Spruce with its short, spiky needles and the Tamarack trees with their branches covered with clumps of soft, greenish needles. These trees had lost their needles in the autumn, but they were now re-growing them. The soft, feathery moss they had just dug up was Sphagnum moss. Labrador tea, a short shrub had rubbery leaves, dull green on top and an orange coloured under side. Old man's beard was the stringy, gray lichen hanging from the dead Black Spruce branches.

"Labrador tea is brewed by many aboriginal people to make a drinking tea. Old man's beard is sometimes used as fire starter," Mabel told the group.

Raymond had tasted the dull, bitter taste of the tea and he had used the old man's beard to start his fire on the island last winter.

"Dried sphagnum moss was used to keep babies dry before diapers," Mabel continued.

"Didn't it stink?"

"No more than regular diapers and the babies didn't get diaper rash because of its antiseptic properties."

Sam told how these wetlands were important ecosystems of the world and why they needed to be preserved.

"In some regions, the decayed moss, called peat, is harvested."

"You can buy bags of peat moss for gardens and stuff," someone said.

"That's right. In some countries they use it for fuel and sometimes they find bodies of animals that have been preserved in the bog for a long time."

"Over here!" Mabel called again.

"This time, find me samples of evidence that animals live in the bog."

This was a bit harder than finding the plants. Most of the animals were hiding, but a squirrel started to chatter. His reddish coloured body shook and his bushy tail bounced erratically as he clung to a tree branch above his midden, next to a pile of spruce cone scales. He had made several tunnels underground where he had stored food. There were lots of middens in this part of the bog.

"Hey! I found some chocolate covered almonds!" Kevin called. Everybody ran to see. A pile of shiny, brown oblong pellets, about the size of a thumb, rested on the spongy moss.

"Those are moose poops!" someone yelled. Everyone laughed.

"Break one apart," Sam told Kevin.

"Yuk!"

"You can use a stick or leaves to handle it, but it won't hurt you."

Sam opened the smooth, rounded, oblong parcel and he showed them the inside.

"Why is there a lot of sawdust?" he asked.

"Because they eat twigs and buds of trees," someone said.

"That's right. Moose are browsers on trees and shrubs."

Others found jagged woodpecker holes where the Pileated Woodpecker had broken out chunks of rotten wood while he was looking for ants and bugs.

"Yuk! A spider web!"

"A bug!"

Raymond knew a lot about the bog, but he didn't want to stand out to show off. No one had teased him with an Indian joke yet, so he just kept quiet.

Mable and Sam called everyone together and they explained the cultural practice of leaving an offering, usually a pinch of tobacco, placed in four directions. This was to thank the Creator for allowing them to take a plant or animal, to take only what was needed.

"Okay," Mabel said. "Find an open space between the Black Spruce trees that's not covered with Labrador tea. Lift the moss and you'll find the longest and straightest spruce roots underneath. Pull up some of these roots and cut them off. We can take a few without hurting the tree and if we harvest carefully, there will be lots left for other times. Also, if you find wads of spruce gum on the trees, carefully cut them off and put them in your bag."

Everyone ran to a different area to harvest roots.

"Ohooo!" someone yelled. "I stepped in a water hole!"

More than one person had wet feet, but everyone was having a good time learning about the bog.

"Time to go!" Sam called. "Back to the bus!"

Everyone grabbed his pile of spruce roots and headed to the bus.

Raymond found a shortcut and he ran to beat the others. He dodged the old man's beard that was hanging down and he jumped from one clump of moss to another.

Sploosh!!

"Help!" Gurgle, gurgle, gasp!

Raymond had dropped into a water hole. The icy water swirled around his body and over his head. He couldn't see because of all the stinking, rotten moss and the tangle of spruce roots.

Grab the roots!

Hang on!

Maybe I should just let go. It's too hard trying to be Indian and a white man.

Noooooo!

I don't want to die!

Don't leave me! I don't want to be preserved in some peat bog!

CHAPTER 3

Raymond still had so many questions. Had Grandpa drowned when his dog sled sank into open water? Maybe Grandpa just gave up on life. Maybe it was too hard trying to be Indian and a white man. Mother gave up her Indian ways and Marg was struggling to hang onto the old ways by the oxbow. Raymond didn't know what to do. Maybe he should just give up.

Nooooooo!
Pull! Pull hard!
Splash! Grunt! Gasp! Sputter! Gag! Puke!
"Help!" Raymond yelled, but no one came.
They're going to leave me.
When Raymond gave the last heave-ho on the roots above,

his body swished through the water hole and he pulled himself up onto the floating mat of moss. Grabbing onto a tree, he made his way to another clump of moss and he found his way back to the trail.

"What on earth happened to you?" Mabel gasped when she saw the soggy, smelly, dripping mass of moss hanging around Raymond's neck as he staggered and shivered toward her.

"I found a water hole," Raymond sputtered.

"Get on the bus and we'll turn on the heaters to keep you from getting hypothermia."

Raymond slowly swung his heavy foot onto the bus. Water ran down the steps as he squished it from his shoes with every step.

"Raymond, you stink!" someone yelled.

"How did you get so wet?" Hilda asked.

Raymond didn't say anything. He just wanted to be left alone. He wanted to remain the shy, quiet Indian kid, yet, since going under the water, there was a spark of incentive to change.

Some day I'd like to talk to that girl. I guess today isn't a good time.

Raymond could hardly stand the smell, himself. He couldn't stop shaking. Leaving soggy footprints along the way, he found his way to the back of the bus. As he huddled by the back seat heater, he found himself alone and depressed.

How could I be such a klutz? It's not like I try to get into trouble, but trouble seems to find me. I nearly killed my brother when I crashed the one thing that really made me happy. That snowmobile is still a pile of junk sitting at Marg's. I don't know if my Grandfather is alive or dead. He probably disappeared because of some curse on Dog Island. My real father is trapping somewhere in the bush up North, and my

Cree mother acts like a white woman. Marg, my kohkom, seems like the only one who understands me and half the time, I can't understand her. Why am I so mixed up?

"Turn down the heat!" someone yelled. "I'm going to throw up!"

"Yeah, the smell is getting pretty bad."

Finally, the bus pulled into the schoolyard. Everyone, except Raymond, piled out. He could hardly move. His muscles were stiff and his wet clothes and jacket weighed him down.

"Sorry for the mess," Raymond told the bus driver as he sloshed down the steps.

"Are you going to be okay?" Sam asked, before he left with the other kids.

"Yeah."

Everyone watched as Raymond made his way to his locker. He tried to remember his lock numbers.

"Hey, Indian! You stink!" a red haired girl yelled. Everyone laughed.

The redhead was Arlene and her blond friend was Susan. They often hung around with Larry and his white friends.

Just as Raymond went by, he swung his head hard and the muskeg water streamed from his pony tail and hit the redhead in the face.

"Now, who stinks?" Raymond mumbled.

No one made Indian jokes in the bush, but as soon as I get to school, the redhead and her gang start in on me. But, hey, I sure let her have it.

Raymond had to laugh, as he realized how he had reacted to the gang. The water hadn't hurt anyone, yet he had stood up for himself.

Maybe, being Indian isn't so bad.

Raymond got his dry gym shirt, shorts, sweat pants, and runners and he headed for the boys' shower room. Warm water coursed down his brown body. Soap in his hair helped take out some of the stench.

At least I'm not shivering anymore.

I've got to get home. I need to go to Marg's tonight to look after the dogs. Grandpa had to look after dogs to make a living. I can do it just for fun.

"Hey, Raymond! What are you doing here so late?" Jack called.

"It's a long story," Raymond said, as he finished up at his locker and pulled out his math homework. His wet clothes were in the garbage can.

I don't want to flunk.

"Hey, Jack. You want to go with me to take care of the dogs?"

"Okay, but I have to be back in time for the hockey game. We're in the play-offs and tonight's a big game."

"No problem. It won't take long. We'll just run by my house to get some dog food and head to Old Town."

"Okay."

Jack is my good friend and he'll understand when I tell him what happened today. It's actually quite funny, but I could have drowned.

Raymond shuddered at the thought.

"Run, white man!" Raymond yelled to Jack as they raced along the trail leading to Old Town. Raymond wouldn't say this to just any white man, but he knew Jack would laugh.

"You have genes for running," Jack gasped. "I like hockey better. We get to sit on the bench half the time. Ha!"

"Look at the icebergs," Raymond pointed out. "The lake is breaking up and the chunks are floating down the river."

"They're going to get caught at the weir."

"Maybe Old Town will flood again, as in the olden days."

Spring had come to Slave Lake and the usual events were taking place. The air had a clean feel to it as the winter sludge was melting and being swept away down the Lesser Slave River. This river was the only outlet for the large lake.

"Look at the black and white ducks!" Raymond called as the boys ran along the oxbow to Marg's cabin.

"What kind are they?" Jack asked.

"Mostly Goldeneyes and Mergansers. They are the first to come north after break up."

"What is there to eat this time of year?"

"They dive for the small fish swimming in the lake and river. There should be some big Northern Pike coming into the oxbow."

"Tundra Swans!" Raymond called out.

"They make a beautiful, white V against the blue sky," Jack observed.

The swans were all white and they were much bigger than Snow Geese. Snow Geese had black wing tips. Canada Geese were dark gray with a white chin stripe.

"I love spring," Raymond said to no one in particular.

At last he could forget about Math, muskeg water and slurs from the redhead.

"Run!" Raymond yelled, as he headed for Marg's cabin. A white, puffy curl of smoke swirled from the old, rusty chimney that had soot marks along the side. Black smoke was coming from another small shed near the oxbow.

"The shed's on fire!" Jack yelled.

"No, that's the smoke house."

"Must be a lot of Marg's friends in there smoking."

"Marg is smoking some fish. Maybe we can get something to eat."

"Tânsí," Raymond called. He was practicing some of the Cree words he had learned from Marg.

"Shadow!" Raymond sputtered as a white husky jumped up and licked his face. Shadow the Second was the offspring of Raymond's grandfather's lead dog. Marg and Raymond were raising Shadow and two other dogs. Raymond wanted to train them to be sled dogs.

"Down!" Raymond scolded, as the dogs mobbed the boys. They could smell the bag of dog food under Raymond's arm and they knew it was chow time.

"Barf! What is that wretched smell?"

"That's the pile of fish guts."

Partly decomposed fish carcasses, with their guts and eyeballs hanging out, were draped across a heap of bones and dried skin. The dogs ate some fresh cleanings, but they wouldn't touch this stuff. It was too rotten.

Raymond gave a whistle as he opened the bag. He was training the dogs to respond to his whistle and his voice, since they needed to obey his directions if they were going to be sled dogs.

"Here you go."

Raymond dumped some of the dried dog food into their dishes. Next, he pointed toward a big iron kettle.

"Pull the lid off and grab that shovel," Raymond directed Jack.

"What's in there? I'm not sure I want to know."

"Marg boils some of the fish for the dogs and we mix it with the dry food. Shovel a bit into each dog dish."

"Wow! They sure like that stuff."

The dogs grabbed and snarled as they devoured the mangled fish bodies.

"Âstom," Marg called from the smoke house. "Come here."

As she opened the door of the smoke house, the boys could see rows of fish fillets hanging over some poles. The smoke from the green, willow branches curled around the reddish slabs of Northern Pike and the white fillets of Walleye. The fire could only smolder because, if it got too hot, the fish would cook. Marg's fire was just right to smoke and to dry the fillets.

"Pe mîcisok" Marg said as she handed each of the boys a chunk of well smoked fish and a piece of bannock she had just taken from a pan on the fire.

"I don't know about this," Jack sighed, as he hesitated

before taking a bite of the fish. The bannock looked good with its crusty, golden, outer shell and soft, steamy, white centre. The smell of fresh baked bread made his salivary glands start working.

"Thanks," Raymond said to Marg, as he took a big bite of the bannock and then he broke off a piece of the well smoked fish. He didn't realize how hungry he was. He had used up a lot of energy today, with all the shivering in the cold water and running from school to Old Town. The rich, brown-coloured, smoked fish fillet had a pleasant smell of smoldering willow and birch and it broke apart into beautiful white sections, with its herring bone pattern of neatly arranged parcels of tender meat. The smoke taste blended with the fish taste and made a scrumptious combination. Marg had filleted the fish so that there were no bones.

"Wow! Marg, you sure know how to cook."

"I've been a good kohkom for a long time now," Marg said with a bit of a grin and a chuckle.

I love her sense of humour. Maybe it's an aboriginal thing. We do like to laugh.

"What is wrong with you?" Raymond called to Jack.

Jack had wandered off to the other side of the smoke house.

"It's just that every time I get the fish close to my mouth, I see that pile of fish guts."

"Oh, come on! Just eat it! It's great!"

"You'd better take those dogs for a run," Marg instructed. "Here. Tie some chunks of wood to these old harness straps and then put the harnesses on the dogs."

"Okay."

"Jack! Bring those straps over here."

"Down!" Raymond told the dogs.

Raymond did not yell at the dogs. He tried to work with them in a calm fashion to make them follow his commands.

"They need to get used to a harness and to learn to pull things," Raymond informed Jack. "We start out with thin straps and a small chunk of wood. They are at the right age to start learning to pull. We'll soon be able to hook them together and then to train them to pull a small, lightweight toboggan."

"How do they know what you want them to do?"

"We have certain commands that they have to learn. We use them over and over and then we reward them when they get it right. It will take a long time. Marg is working with them during the day. 'Hike' means to get moving. 'Gee' is to turn right. 'Haw' is left. 'Easy' is to slow down. 'Whoa' to stop."

"I don't think these dogs will ever learn all that, but they sure want to pull."

"That is part of their breeding. Shadow is from the old dog over there. She's Storm. She came from my grandpa's dog team. My Shadow looks like Grandpa's lead dog, Shadow. He is Alaskan husky which isn't actually a breed. It is a mixture of the Alaskan malamute, a big, strong dog and Siberian husky, which is a smaller, faster dog. Shadow has the typical white coat with blue eyes. The other two are real mongrels."

"Where is your Grandpa's Shadow?" Jack asked.

"I don't know, exactly, what happened to Grandpa and his Shadow," Raymond said. "They say he and Shadow disappeared in a blizzard on Dog Island."

"That's too bad."

"That's why I want to go to the island. Maybe I can find some clues. Mother and Allen tell me not to go to Dog Island and I think Marg believes there is some kind of curse on the island. She doesn't say much about it."

"Is that where you crashed your snowmobile?"

"Yeah. That's that pile of junk over there. Larry and I crashed before we got to the island and then I had to look after his broken leg. I dragged him home on the hood of the snowmobile. There was no chance to explore the island and besides, it was pretty spooky over there."

"Will you go to the island again, if you can get your snowmobile fixed?"

"I don't know. I haven't had time to work on it. Maybe I can go back by boat this summer."

The dogs were restless and they wanted to run. Raymond and Jack had to hold them back as they fastened the harnesses, with the chunks of wood, to the dogs.

This is fun. I like working with the dogs. I can do the same things Grandpa did. I can be proud to have had a mosôm like him.

"Whoa! Whoa!" Raymond called.

Too late. The dogs were already headed down the trail along the oxbow.

"I've got to go!" Jack yelled to Raymond.

"Okay. I'll see you at the game."

"Whoa!" Raymond called after the dogs.

What a mess! They're all tangled up and they've run off on me. How will I ever make a dog team out of them? How did Grandpa train his dogs?

Raymond could hear the yelping of the pups in the distance. He struggled through some patches of snow and ice, heading into the muskeg.

No! I don't want to go there!

Raymond followed the tracks of the dogs, calling as he went. They went through some grassy meadows, with the green blades just starting to show. He jumped from one clump to the next, realizing that there was water near to the surface.

Then the trail turned and headed into the thick stands of Black Spruce and Tamarack.

No! Not again!

"Shadow! Cocoa! Sarge!"

It's no use! I'll never find them! How could I be so stupid as to let them run off?

What's that? A cry of a coyote? What if the coyote lures the pups away and then attacks them? They say a coyote will do that. What am I going to say to Marg?

Raymond made his way back toward Marg's cabin and the smoke house, with the curls of smoke lifting skyward. On the other side of the meadow, a shallow lake came into view. He had never seen this before.

This looks like a big horseshoe.

Trip! Thunk! Raymond tripped and he fell on a big clump of grass. His foot had caught on a chain of some sort.

What is this?

Raymond slowly pulled the chain and he found it attached to a nearly completely rotted chunk of wood.

It looks like part of a dog chain. How did this chain get over here? Would Grandpa have had dogs tied up over here? It's a long way from the cabin. Maybe Marg will know.

Marg! Oh yeah, I'll have to tell her about the dogs.

CHAPTER 4

"Where are the dogs?" Marg asked as Raymond limped in with his stubbed toe. His pride was hurt more than his toe.

"I lost them."

"How could you do that?"

"They ran off and I think a coyote lured them into a trap. They're probably getting chewed to pieces right now."

"Don't worry. It's okay. They can look after themselves. Remember, they can be tough if they need to be and they are strong."

"Marg, I'm really mixed up. There are so many things happening. I don't know what's going to happen next."

"Teenage years can be that way. Can I help?"

Raymond related some of the events of the day. Tears came to his eyes as he recalled the feeling he had in the water and on the bus.

"Can I ask you a few questions about Grandpa?"
"Go ahead."
"What kind of boat did Grandpa have? Did he ever have a skin boat?"
"Your mosôm never had a skin boat. He built his own birch bark canoe, but he put some modern things on it as well. He used common, metal tools to make the work easier than in the olden days. Some people covered the canoe frame with canvas."
"I had a dream about Grandpa being attacked by warriors when he was poling a skin boat."

Raymond related his bad dream to Kohkom. He had still remembered every frightening detail.

"Sometimes our people have spirit dreams" Marg said. Your dream was from before Mosôm's time. If that had been real, you would have been one of the warriors. Moose hide boats were used a long time ago. My kohkom told me that the first people in this area were the Beaver and Slavey. That was where the name Slave Lake came from. A rather peace-loving people, they used skin boats to cross rivers and streams. These boats were only temporary, since the skin soon started to rot and they weren't used on the open water of big lakes."

Marg put a frying pan on the old, blackened wood cook stove. She stirred the ashes and got a crackling fire going with a new piece of birch wood. A curl of smoke drifted into the air. Raymond loved the smell of wood smoke, which blended with the dry wood smell of the old log cabin.

"Woodland Cree took over Slave Lake when they came West looking for fur," Marg continued. "We had lots of fur animals around here. There were even herds of buffalo (bison), especially on the plains near the west end of the lake. Today, that area is called Buffalo Bay. Some say the Slavey used fire to keep the grass growing."

"Why would they want to set their land on fire?"

"Fire burns off the old, dead grass and makes way for new grass to grow. It also kills shrubs and trees that would soon take over."

"Why did the Cree have nice canoes and the others have only rough, skin boats?"

"Birch bark canoes came from the East," Marg said as she put a big slab of fish into the sizzling frying pan. Grease from the pan spattered onto the top of the stove and this added another smoke smell to the air.

I'm sooo hungry. I hope she has some for me.

"Were they Algonquins?" Raymond asked.

"I guess so, but the Cree made changes so their canoes would handle better on the northern waters."

Marg flipped the fish over and she kept talking.

"Eventually, the Cree drove all the other tribes up North and they took over their lands. Some of those people still live in northern Alberta. Small pox and other diseases killed a lot of our people in the early days."

"How did Mosôm learn to make canoes?"

"I don't know, but probably he learned from his father. He always made his own canoes ever since I knew him. The birch bark canoes were used for hauling furs and supplies. Our people worked hard paddling the canoes and boats for the traders. They also spent a lot of time and hard work building canoes."

I can be proud to be an Indian.

"We are starting to build a canoe at school."

"Yes, your father, Johnny, brought a roll of birch bark from up north. He dropped it off and said it was for you," Marg said, as she sliced some potatoes and carrots into the pan with the fish.

I am sooo hungry. The sides of my stomach are doing somersaults and my liver is doing a high dive.

Marg took the lid off a pan and she wound a swatch of bannock onto a stick.

"Here. Take this to the fireplace and roast it. You're going to stay to eat, aren't you?"

Raymond wanted to yell, "YES!", but he just said, "Thanks. I should be able to. Mom knows I often eat here when I come to take care of the dogs."

"Âstome. The fish is ready for eating."

"This bannock is perfect. Thank you sooo much. I'm starving."

"Raymond, you're always starving," Marg said with her usual chuckle.

That big slab of fish, with its browned edges and flaky sections, soon triggered Raymond's taste buds and the tender meat satisfied his hunger. The crisp, tender, golden carrots and the almost charred, grease-coated potatoes had just the right texture. It didn't take long for him to devour the smoked fish, the veggies and the bannock, with its dripping, sticky swirls of honey.

"Wow!" Raymond exclaimed, as he cleaned his plate with his honey bannock to get every last morsel. "That was sooo good! I think you cookum better every day!"

"I try."

"Have you ever been to the lake that looks like a horseshoe?"

"No, but that is what the old people called it, Horseshoe Lake."

"Did Mosôm ever go there?"

"No, he stayed away from that lake because he said there were bad spirits there."

"Why? What was wrong with it?"

"I don't know. He never said, but I think somebody got killed over there."

"Did anyone live there?"

"In the olden days, there were two trading posts in this area, the North West post and the Hudson's Bay post, called Fort Waterloo. They didn't like each other so they were always fighting. A lot of furs were traded for booze. Sometimes, there were arguments about prices. People got mad and started fighting"

That sounds interesting. I should check that out.

"Do you think a relative died over there?"

"I don't know. Some people may have died in a big fight between the people at the North West and the Hudson's Bay posts. They even burned down some of the buildings near Horseshoe Lake. That was a long time ago."

"Have you ever found any part of the old buildings over there?"

"No. I stay by the oxbow. I don't have time to go digging around for stuff."

"Have you ever seen a chain like this?" Raymond asked, as he showed Marg the short chain he had found. "I tripped on this and stubbed my toe on an old chunk of wood."

"You do have a lot of questions."

"This looks like a piece of dog chain," Marg said, after she had cleaned off more of the dirt.

"That's what I thought. Do you see the markings on it?"

"I can't see very well, but it looks like some initial."

"Would that be Grandpa's? It looks like an "A" scratched into the metal. That could be for Alphonse. Could this be his dog chain?"

"Now, you're thinking crazy. Stop snooping around over there. That stuff is from the olden days."

"Do you hear the pups?"

"They must be getting hungry again. I told you they would be okay."

Time! Time for the hockey game.

"Thanks for everything. I have to go. You're a great kohkom."

"You're getting to be a pretty good looking grandson. When are you going to braid that ponytail?" Marg asked with a chuckle. "Don't forget the birch bark."

Raymond untangled the pups and scolded them for running off on him. They were soon into the food dishes.

"Maybe they're ready for the toboggan," Marg called, as Raymond headed for town.

"Ekosi. See you tomorrow."

Raymond still had questions about Grandpa and the mystery on Dog Island, but he was feeling much better about being an Indian.

CHAPTER 5

I stayed too long at Marg's, but I learned a lot. These thoughts filled Raymond's mind as he ran toward the bridge.

I'm going to be late for the game, but I have to stop on the bridge.

Raymond took in the sights and sounds of the river flowing beneath the bridge. The smell of the fresh air coming from the lake perked up his lungs and spirit. In the southwestern sky, daylight lingered, as the days were getting longer.

Wow! What a view! I should have a camera!

Streaks of yellow and golden light pierced through breaks in dark blue clouds on the horizon and shrouded Dog Island with mysterious shadows. Raymond felt drawn to the island. He knew he had a strange connection, since his grandfather had disappeared on the island. Raymond wanted to go back to the island to find out more about that connection.

This is better than a hockey game. I'd like to stay longer, but I promised Jack I'd watch him play in the big game.

The ice tinkled, as the slivers of ice clinging to different ice chunks, bumped into one another and splintered the candle-like pieces into the cold, black water which flowed from the lake and headed north to the Arctic.

In the water, male Goldeneye ducks swam around the females. As they shook their heads from side-to-side, showing off their greenish heads that contrasted with the bright black and white markings on their backs, Raymond watched.

They don't seem to be shy around girls like I am. They're not Indian.

Sometimes, several males were interested in the same female and then they would try to chase each other off by pecking, splashing and squawking at the intruder. Some ducks had already partnered when they arrived in Slave Lake, but most of the mating and nesting occurred farther north.

Wow! That was close.

A flock of ducks swished low over the bridge, piercing the dim light, casting shimmering shadows on the surface of the water. A whistling sound identified the Goldeneye, sometimes called whistlers. When they landed feet first in the water, a sound like a distant motor boat, echoed up from the river.

I've got to go, Raymond thought, as the last glimmer of sunshine slipped beneath the horizon. Raymond headed for home. Gasping for air, but not stopping to rest, he grabbed open the heavy, creaking garage door and he threw the bundle of birch bark onto the cracked, cluttered floor. No one was home so he took off running again.

The pounding of his heart seemed to keep time with the pounding of his feet as he picked up his pace, heading down the street to the ice arena. As he raced into the parking lot, his nostrils rebelled against the putrid, black, diesel smoke from the motor coach that was sitting in front of the entrance.

I guess the visiting team is here.

What a contrast this was to the river scene, with its peaceful sights and sounds. Here was the sound of urban confusion, the roar of the bus, the traffic noises of cars trying to find parking spots, kids and adults shouting to one another across the lot, and the slamming of heavy arena doors.

Yuk! Greasy hamburgers.

The smells of the concession area greeted Raymond at the door as he lined up with others to pay and to get a stamp on his hand. Burger grease and fried onions spread their presence throughout the entrance. Hoping to get a burger and pop, little kids ran to the concession stand. Parents scrambled to harness the kids, to pay for the tickets, to enter the daily raffle and to look to see if their sons were in the starting lineup. Everyone hurried to get to the bleachers alongside the oval ice rink, hoping to get his favorite spot next to friends who would join him in cheering and noise making.

"Yuk," Raymond said, as he stuck his head into the home dressing room looking for Jack. Body odour, mixed with the stink of sweaty socks, shoulder pads, knee pads, jock straps and jerseys hit the gag reflex.

Jack thought the rotten fish at Marg's smelled bad. This is twice as bad.

"Hi, Raymond," someone yelled. "How's life on the rez?"

"Great! My tepee smells a lot better than this place."

Everyone laughed.

At one time, Raymond would have been ready to fight if someone had said that, but now he had a better understanding of his Indian heritage. He could even joke about it.

Jack, with his head sticking through a hole in his shoulder pads, waved to Raymond. Hockey could get rough, especially in the playoffs and the players needed protective gear. Some players already had their skates tied tight, their helmets and sticks in hand as they skate-walked on the hard rubber floor out to the open gate that allowed them to step onto the ice and to glide away in a smooth, effortless motion.

I'd end up on my butt if I did that. It takes lots of practice to be that good.

Raymond knew Jack had spent hours at the rink doing drills and practicing plays the coach had outlined for the players. Tonight, they had to put it all together as a team if they were going to win against their arch rivals.

I don't want to sit in the middle of the home-town section. It's going to be loud. I don't want to sit in the visitor section either.

Raymond made his way up the bleachers, dodging kids who were running with slopping pop and dripping ketchup. Other teenagers were coming in with blankets and noisemakers. The spectators were warmed from above by electric heaters, but their bums could get cold, sitting on the hard, wooden, gray painted seats.

Here's a spot that is pretty neutral and there is still lots of room.

Raymond scrunched up his long legs and he flexed his back.

It's going to be a long night with leg cramps and a strained back.

There were no backs on these benches and Raymond had to make sure no one had left wet, muddy spots from boots, since the seats were also used as footrests.

RETURN TO DOG ISLAND

It must be getting close to game time. The Zamboni is coming out.

The Zamboni, a propane powered tractor with a mechanized ice shaver and collector on the back, shaved off the old ice, spewed it into a big container on the back as it spread clean water onto the ice surface so it would freeze into a smooth, hard surface to skate on.

"Hey, Jack!" Raymond yelled, as Jack skated onto the ice. Of course, Jack couldn't hear him.

As the home team skated onto the ice for their warm up session, a loud cheer went up. The horns and whistles vibrated the brain and rang throughout the rounded roof section, with its big arching beams. Some cheers and boos greeted the visiting team. The goalies, with their bulky padding, skated back and forth through the crease in front of their nets. The big bladed sticks, and cushioned arm pads, called blockers, helped the goalies to keep the puck from going into the nets behind them.

"Raymond!" someone yelled.

"Hi, Hilda," Raymond replied in a rather startled voice. "What are you doing here?"

"We came to see some Canadian hockey," Hilda said, as she and two other exchange students sat down on the bench with Raymond. Hilda slid over next to Raymond and started chattering away.

I was hoping for a chance to talk with Hilda and now, I'm scared. No worry. I can't get a word in anyway. She doesn't seem to care that I am an Indian.

Everyone was laughing and having a great time. They were excited to see the game of hockey.

"You can tell us about hockey," Hilda said. "You should know a lot about hockey since you are an original Canadian."

I don't know a lot about hockey, but maybe just enough to impress Hilda.

"What do you want to know?"

"How do you play the game?" Hilda asked, her brown eyes flashing and her smooth face breaking into a smile enclosed by strands of flowing, sandy coloured hair.

"Uh, well, each team tries to get the puck in the other team's net."

"They play with puke?"

"No," Raymond laughed, "it's a round, black, hard rubber puck."

"It can't be round; it's sliding."

Well, it is round in one way, but flat in the other."

"But, look. Now it is rolling. How can it roll if it is flat?"

Bang!! A puck came flying over the glass that sits on top of the side-boards.

Someone grabbed it and tossed it to Raymond. They had heard him struggling to explain the puck to Hilda.

"Now, I see," she said as she examined the puck. "It's round one way and flat the other."

"That's what I said."

This is not the kind of talking with Hilda I had in mind, but I kinda like it.

"What are those guys doing skating around in the jail clothes?" someone asked from down the bench.

"They are the refs. They make sure the game is played fair and they give out penalties if someone breaks the rules."

"It looks like a lot of milling around in a confused state to me," another stated.

"Okay," Raymond said. "Here is a short course." In between the cheering and the blasts from the air horn, Raymond tried to explain the basics of the game.

"How do they know when to start?" Hilda asked.

"The players take positions around one of the red circles, with the centres facing one another. The ref drops the puck on the ice and the centre who wins the draw passes it to his team mates and away they go."

"Look, they're starting to introduce the players now."

"Stand up for singing "Oh Canada.""

The crowd screeched, the horns blasted and the puck was dropped at centre ice. No one could ask any more questions.

A few minutes later, Hilda leaned close and asked Raymond, "Why did the ref blow the whistle to stop the game?"

"The home team iced the puck."

"What is that? I thought it was already on ice."

"Well, our team was in trouble so Jack iced the puck."

"Why did he do that?"

"He knew that the other team was ready to score so when he got his stick on the puck, he shot it out of his end. It crossed too many lines without being touched by one of his teammates, so they have to bring it back to our end and have a face off."

"Jack is going off."

"Yeah, he tripped someone and he has to go to the penalty box. See, I told you players get penalties for breaking the rules."

"Jack broke a rule?"

"Yep. No tripping. Now the other team gets a power-play. They can still have five players, but we can only have four."

"That's not fair."

"That's the game."

"Whew! We killed off that penalty. That means they didn't score when we were shorthanded," Raymond explained before she asked. He realized that explaining all of the terms of hockey to Hilda was impossible.

"Who's winning?"

"Well, no one is winning."

"Then, why is everyone cheering?"

"That is the end of the first period and no one scored. There will be two more periods before the game is over and maybe we will score the winning goal."

"It seems rather useless to me, all that skating back and forth and they won't let anyone score."

"That's a good defensive game. You want a burger?"

"Sure."

"Okay. Come."

Raymond, Hilda and the others climbed down the bleachers, fighting the crowd. They talked, laughed and had a good time waiting in line at the concession booth.

CHAPTER 6

The rest of the game was fast and furious. Both teams made great plays and they took lots of shots on net, but the goalies displayed great skill, skating across their creases, stopping shots with their sticks, gloves, and pads. Raymond tried to explain everything to Hilda and the exchange students. They didn't seem too excited, but they cheered whenever Raymond cheered.

"Why do they fight?" Hilda asked. "Isn't that illegal?"

"Well, no. Not in hockey. The refs have to control it and when the fighters get tired out, they get ushered to the penalty boxes to cool off."

Buzzzzz!

"What is that for?" Hilda asked as everyone stood up, cheered and headed for the door again.

"That's the end of the second period."

"You mean we have to stand in line again?"

"No, we can just stand up here and stretch."

"You mean like the seventh inning stretch?" someone said.

"What is that?" Hilda asked.

"It comes after the seventh inning in baseball," another student replied.

Raymond was glad, because he wasn't sure what it was.

As the Zamboni driver made his rounds, someone came by selling tickets on half the house.

"Why is someone selling half of their house at a hockey game?" Hilda wanted to know.

"It's a way to raise money for the teams. Everyone buys a ticket and the winner gets half of all the money that is collected."

"That's neat. It's like giving away your money for fun."

Just then a friendly guy in an Edmonton Oilers' cap came around selling tickets on a raffle for a hockey stick.

"How much?" Raymond asked.

"Fifty dollars."

"Fifty Dollars!" Hilda exclaimed. "Who would pay that much for a stick?"

"This is a special hockey stick. It is autographed by Wayne Gretzky and the money goes to build a new library," the guy said, with a big smile.

"It sounds like a good cause, but I don't have that kind of money," Hilda told him.

"That's okay. I'll bug some of the old, rich guys."

"Why would some guy's signature on a stick be worth that much?" Hilda wanted to know.

"He's a famous hockey player," Raymond said, as the crowd roared again when the teams skated onto the ice for the third period."

"They're going to do it all over again?"

"Yes. This is the last period. Hopefully, we will score a goal."

Back and forth, the players skated. Some looked tired and sweat stains streaked their sweaters. The game was coming down to the final minutes.

"Now!" Raymond yelled, as Jack skated around the defense.

Long strides propelled Jack toward the visitors' goalie. He was going in alone. No whistles. It was now or never. Everyone was screaming, "SHOOT!" At the last second, Jack faked a shot to the goalie's right shoulder and then he pushed the puck between the goalie's leg pads and into the back of the net. The red light lit up and the horns blew.

There was screaming, yelling, back slapping, and hugging. The home team was happy and Jack was a hero. The visiting spectators were quiet for a change.

Two minutes were left in the game. The opposing coach decided to pull his goalie in hopes of getting the tying goal before time ran out. All of the spectators stood up and started chanting and stomping their feet. Tension was high. The players skated back and forth on tired legs, their bodies aching from all of the checking and fighting that had taken place. No one wanted to take a penalty and the refs didn't want to stop the flow of the game. There were hard hitting body checks and poke checks at the puck and the visitors took lots of slapshots at the home team's goalie. The five home team players had to keep the six visiting players from scoring.

The fans were yelling, clapping and pushing to get a better view. Hilda covered her ears to stop the noise. This was hockey in Canada!

With fours seconds left on the clock, Jack managed to get the puck. He slapped it past a defenseman and banked it off the boards. The puck slid undefended into the visitors' net. The red light went on. The horns blew. Game over!

Bedlam erupted in the stands. Bedlam erupted on the ice. The home players mobbed Jack. Onto the ice, they all fell in a heap. The home goalie skated over and piled on, crushing everyone with his heavy equipment. The visiting players skated to their bench, tired and dejected about losing the game, in a shutout. The visiting spectators, stunned by the loss, were still willing to cheer for both teams as they lined up to shake hands. Then, they all skated to their locker rooms.

"Jack's a hero!" Raymond yelled.

"Why?" Hilda asked.

"He had the winning goal and then he put the game away with the puck in the empty net."

"Great! Now, I know all about Canadian Hockey."

"Let's wait for the crowd to clear. I want to wait to congratulate Jack anyway."

Mass confusion reigned as the home team finally came out of the locker room and met with friends and family. Hugs, backslapping and cheers greeted the winning team. They were going to the finals.

At last, Jack came over to see Raymond and the exchange students.

"How did you like Canadian hockey?"

"Great!" everyone cheered.

As they went to the parking lot, someone yelled, "Hey, moose poops!"

Raymond looked around, thinking someone was calling to him.

Out of the dark, a small aboriginal boy pounced on a bigger white boy. Fists were flying and boots were kicking. There was blood, but no weapons.

"Look after this," Jack said, as he looked at Hilda and motioned toward his hockey bag and stick.

"Raymond!" Jack called. "I'll take the white man and you take the Indian."

"Okay! Okay! That's enough!" Raymond yelled as they separated the smaller boys. Jack started the white kid on his way, telling him to mind his mouth.

Raymond knew the aboriginal boy. His name was Mel Moostoos. Everyone called him "M and M" for short, but some kids called him "moose poops" in a taunting way because of his aboriginal name.

"Hey, M and M. What's going on?" Raymond asked as he tried to calm the young boy. "It's okay to be an Indian. You can be proud of your name. Your great, great grandfather Moostoos was a great leader. He signed the first treaty for this area called Treaty Eight. We can all be proud of him. If someone calls you moose poops again, just say môniyâw, whiteman, and walk away. Now, get out of here and head for home."

Raymond realized that what he had said was true for himself, as well as for M and M. They could both be proud of their grandparents. It made Raymond feel good to be able to help this Indian boy.

"Picking on little boys again?"

It was the redhead talking and giggling with her white friends.

"He's my friend," Raymond said, not bothering to look at the scrawny kid who was always giving him trouble. Now, he felt bad again.

When the crowd had left, Raymond and Jack returned to their friends.

"Ready to go?" Jack asked.

Raymond was just going to say, "okay", when Hilda stepped forward and picked up the hockey stick. Jack swung his bag onto his shoulder.

"See ya around," Jack said, as the two headed off.

"Thanks for explaining hockey to me," Hilda said. "Jack said you would tell me all about it. See you in class."

"Yah," was all Raymond could say. He felt as if someone had kicked him square in the guts.

Raymond headed for home by himself and the hockey hero walked off with Hilda.

"Aarrgh!" Raymond yelled into the night, as he kicked at a chunk of ice on the side of the road.

"Ouch!" Pain shot through the toe that he had stubbed at Marg's.

Why am I so stupid! How can things go so bad so quick? Five minutes ago, I thought I was making friends with Hilda. Now, she is off with my best friend, my toe is thumping with pain and that redhead and her friends are making fun of me again.

"Owwww!"

Phantom wings beat quietly against the black sky as a flock of Tundra Swans flew overhead.

I wish I could fly north with them. If I could find Grandpa on the island, we could go north together.

CHAPTER 7

Trip! Slip! Bounce, bounce.

"Noooooo!" Raymond said as the roll of birch bark slipped from under his arm and bounced and rolled down the hall of the school. His math book skidded across the floor.

I wanted to get this to the CTS room unnoticed and now I've become an Indian spectacle again.

"Hey, Raymond!" someone called. "That's gonna make a big moose caller. Maybe you'll call up a heap big bull moose."

"Maybe a grizzly bear," another said.

I should have known. It's the redhead gang again.

It was true. Birch bark was sometimes rolled into a V-shaped megaphone to make the human voice sound like a moose call or grunt. It was true that if the call was good enough to call a moose, it could also attract predators of the moose.

Dejectedly, Raymond gathered up the birch bark and he retrieved his math book. He wanted to kick the math book because he hadn't done his homework again. After he had spent a lot of time thinking about Hilda and Jack last night, Math was the last thing he wanted to do.

Raymond headed for the CTS room, trying not to hit anyone with his big roll of birch bark. Talking and laughing students, all scrambling to their rooms before the bell rang, crowded the hall.

I'll pile this on top of the other rolls. It looks like I'm not the only one who brought birch bark.

Some students had fathers who worked in forestry who had cut birch wood for their fireplaces. They knew where the large trees were and they peeled the bark off before they chain-sawed the logs into smaller chunks for firewood.

Mable and Sam must have been here already. Some of the bark has been soaked and steamed.

The day dragged on for Raymond. Another story was given for him to write in English class. More theorems in Math. He ate lunch by himself, since Jack and Hilda had gone out for lunch.

At least the redhead gang isn't around. I just want to think. Where can I get a boat to go to Dog Island this summer to look for signs of Grandpa? Maybe I could build my own birch bark canoe and paddle it to the island. Where can I get enough birch bark? Maybe Marg and father can get more for me. I'm not sure I want to be paddling anything on the lake. That dream was pretty scary!

"Yea! CTS time."

"Hi, Raymond. I liked Canadian hockey, but there were too many fights."

It was Hilda, giving her sly smile as she sauntered by.

With very little feeling, Raymond said, "Glad you liked it."

Raymond wasn't going to be very friendly. Even though he had never made a deliberate, visible show of interest in Hilda before, he felt jilted.

So, it's not her fault. Jack beat me fair and square.

***

"Listen up!" Mabel called.

"The first step today is to come up with a design for the canoe. We need to draw the lines of curvature and to scribe the angles of the bow and stern to make sure they are symmetrical and that they will glide evenly and smoothly through the water. The aboriginal people were able to do this instinctively, but we need to work it out on paper, first. You can actually put some of your geometry to work.

Geometry! Yuk! Grandpa never needed geometry to build his canoes, why should I?

It was easier than Raymond had first thought. Actually, he had a natural feel for drawing the lines, but he was amazed how his geometry helped him understand things better.

Maybe I should do my Math homework. I might even pass that class, if I just put my mind to it. Ha!

Later, the class went outside to the canoe building site. The prepared ground was smooth and somewhat arched, with holes for stakes placed in a way that outlined the general shape of a canoe.

"Okay," Sam instructed, "bring that wet bark and put the white side up."

The students all grabbed onto the bark and they spread it out over the prepared site. It took more than one strip, since one alone was not large enough to cover the whole area. The strips would have to be stitched together later with split spruce roots.

"Alright, grab the gunwale and lay it on the bark," Sam instructed.

The leaders had cheated a little because they had made gunwales ahead of time by cutting thin strips of spruce and bending them under water to get them into the general shape of a canoe. This was the "backbone", running tip to tip along the edge of the canoe. Crosspieces, called thwarts, kept each side of the gunwale at the proper distance to make the correct shape.

"Some of you can put those rocks on the bark to hold it down," Mable said.

"Grab some stakes," Sam called.

"Okay, all together now, move the rocks to the inside and bend the outside of the bark upwards until you can put the stakes in the holes."

"I can't hold on!"

"Don't let it slip!"

"This is hard!"

Raymond and the others worked hard to bring the bark up around the gunwale and to put the stakes into the ground. The stakes from opposite sides were held in place by attaching strings across the bark, making a rather poorly shaped canoe-like structure. The rocks held the gunwale in place on the bottom. Later, the gunwale would be raised and stitched to the top of the birch bark sheets with spruce roots that had been split into halves or quarters. Inside posts would hold the bark in its proper shape to dry. The reddish brown inside of the bark was now on the outside of the canoe, held upright by the two rows of stakes.

"This is hard work!"

Ring. Ring.

"Class is over. See you tomorrow."

***

That evening, Raymond had time to do his math homework.

This isn't so hard. Now I see how it is useful in doing things like building canoes and other things. I can pass this class after all.

Later, Raymond had a dream about a canoe, but it was a good dream. He had built his own canoe and gone to Dog Island to learn all about an ancient civilization that had been living there. Some aboriginal men were chipping rocks to make arrow heads, choppers and scrapers. Others were making primitive tools from bone, antlers, hide and wood. Women were cooking over the open fires next to the tepees. Hides were being scraped and tanned. Furs were being stretched and dried. Over a smoky fire, moose meat hung, drying to become part of pemmican. Raymond saw some men smoking the pipe. Others started drumming, singing and dancing. He felt right at home singing with the drummers and he joined the large circle of dancers doing the off-beat shuffle of the round dance.

More people started dancing. The drums got louder. The dancing got stronger and faster. It rose to a furious pace and then it happened. A young maiden came up to Raymond and started dancing in front of him. Long red hair. Flashing hazel eyes. Red freckles. Glinting metal braces on her teeth.

"Braces! Nooo! Not the redhead!"

"Wake up you crazy Indian!" Larry yelled.

CHAPTER 8

"Listen up!" the leaders called. "Today, we have to finish fastening the birch bark to the gunwales. We have to cut some slits into the bark along the sides and to take out V-shaped pieces of bark called gores. This allows us to fold all of the bark up around the sides with little overlap and to fasten it to the gunwales. We will then stitch the slits together. Any questions?"

"Okay. Let's have at it," Sam encouraged.

***

It took several classes to fasten the bark to the gunwales, to stitch the overlaps and to fit the sheeting into the bottom and the sides of the canoe. Again, Sam and Mable cheated a bit. They had cut thin strips of wood and trimmed them so they would fit snugly into the bottom and sides, following the shape of the canoe. More thin strips, called ribs, were placed across the sheeting and pressed into place every twenty centimetres or so, along the gunwales. The thwarts were fastened permanently to the gunwales. Inside gunwales, birch bark and outside gunwales were all lashed together with spruce roots to hold the bark firmly in place and to make a solid structure.

"Hold this stem piece," Sam instructed the students.

The stem piece was a narrow strip of wood, cut into several laminations and bent in a gentle curve to form the end of the canoe.

"Bring the snips."

"Why are you cutting the birch bark?" Hilda asked.

"Now, we have to trim the bark to match the curve of the stem piece. This all gets lashed together and is fitted in-between the bottom of the canoe and the gunwales to make a strong, narrow end. Some of the early canoes had really fancy stem pieces curving out in front of the canoe. This piece would identify which tribe it belonged to."

"How's the headboard coming?" Mabel asked Raymond.

Mabel had asked Raymond to design the headboard for the canoe. She knew he had some artistic ability and this was a chance for him to show it.

"I've put the sketches on the board. Now, I have to burn them in."

"Wow!" Hilda exclaimed as Raymond showed them the headboard. "You're an Indian artist."

"It's not so great. I actually used my geometry set to scribe some of the circles and ellipses."

"But the Indian in the canoe?"

"Yeah, that is the old man of my dream."

"Wow! You're good."

I'm just doing what I like to do and I guess I'm good at it.

Raymond took the headboard home and he used a metal tool to burn the sketch into the wood. The headboard was an elliptical piece of wood that stood upright between the bottom end of the stem piece and the first thwart that connected the left and right gunwales. It strengthened the front of the canoe and gave shape to the pieces of bark that passed on each side.

"Not bad," Raymond said as he finished the sketch and put some varnish on the wood. "It will be ready for tomorrow."

How about that. Saved by a geometry set and a wild dream.

The next day, Raymond gave the head piece to Marg.

"This is beautiful!" she exclaimed.

"Wow! It is beautiful," they all agreed.

"Great Indian artist," Hilda put in.

It was beautiful, with the sketch of an Indian paddling a canoe across a lake. Circles and elliptical lines swirled out behind the canoe and paddle as it headed for a distant island. The blackened sketch blended into the soft, natural hues of the wood.

"Okay! Okay!" Sam called. "Time to get to work. We have to put that headboard in the front of the canoe."

"Some of you need to help me," Mable said. "We have to start working on the spruce pitch."

"What do we do?"

"Well, the Cree used bear grease and ashes to temper the spruce gum, but we're going to use lard and charcoal."

"Yuk!"

"We have to heat these gobs of spruce gum and then work in the grease and charcoal to make a pitch pliable enough to put on the seams of the canoe."

Both groups worked on their tasks.

"Okay," Sam called. "Now you guys can do the other end of the canoe. I'll watch. Raymond, you're in charge."

"Gulp! What do I know about it?"

"You're the best worker here. Now get to it."

Raymond was a hard worker and he had paid attention when Sam was working on his headboard, but he didn't consider himself to be a leader. He liked to stay in the background. Raymond wasn't sure what to do, but then he said, "Okay you guys, grab the other headboard and the snips."

"Ow!"

"This is hard work!"

"I broke my nail," Hilda complained.

Raymond had to chuckle at all of the complaining.

This is hard work, but nothing like what Grandfather had to do when he was a young boy. I liked doing the headboard and we did a good job.

"Okay, finish the spruce stitching and we'll soon be ready for the pitch. Don't wear good clothes tomorrow," Sam instructed.

***

That night, on the way to Marg's, Raymond stopped at the town library. He wasn't familiar with the place, since he only used it once in awhile when he had a school project. In a shy, quiet voice, he asked the librarian about the history of Slave Lake. With a friendly smile, she showed him several books in the local history section. He wanted to find something about the history of Slave Lake and Dog Island. He didn't have much time, but what he saw sparked his interest.

***

Raymond found Marg in the kitchen. As he swung a long leg over a well worn, wooden chair, with scratches along the sides, and perched on it backwards, he decided to ask Marg some more questions about the olden days.

"Did you ever ride on the Northern Light?" Raymond asked Marg.

"What? Do you think I am that old?"

"Well?"

"Ha! That was an old time paddle wheeler steamship that traveled on the lake. My mother told of seeing it go by when she was a little girl, but she didn't mix much with that kind. The travelers were a mixture of gold diggers, homesteaders and high society folks.

"Did Grandpa ever live on Dog Island in the olden days?"

"Not that I know of," Marg said as she slapped a piece of moose meat into a hot frying pan on the old cook stove. The curls of steam and the smells of the searing meat touched off Raymond's hunger pangs.

Not again! I'm going crazy from hunger."

"The captain of the ship lived on the island and he had a bit of a farm there. I hear he entertained the high society folks with tea parties and such. Our folks worked with the freight and stuff, but we wouldn't have been invited for tea. Now, you tend to the dogs before I lose patience with all of your questions."

Raymond loved the dogs and they were starting to listen to his commands. Shadow, the white husky snuggled for attention. Cocoa, the dark brown dog with one drooping ear, stood at attention, just waiting to snatch the treat Raymond always tossed. Sarge, the black and white Border collie, spun round and round and back and forth, always ready to give chase to something.

They're going to make a great team.

"Hike!" Raymond called as the dogs took off on their nightly run. Raymond ran alongside, giving directions, as the dogs pulled a makeshift toboggan in preparation for the real thing in the near future.

Maybe someday I'll be a dog musher like my Grandpa. That would be something I could be proud of.

"Penâta! Come and get it!" Marg called, as Raymond untied the dogs and let them go for a drink. "Moose meat's ready."

"Mmmm! This is sooo good. I love moose meat and bannock."

"You love food, period!" Marg laughed.

"When did Grandpa start trapping on Dog Island?"

"Enough questions about Dog Island. Take this bannock and awas. Ekosi. See you tomorrow?"

"I'll have more questions about the olden days."

"Awas," Marg gurgled in her laughing way, but Raymond sensed she was serious about not answering any more questions about Dog Island.

Why is everybody afraid to talk about Grandpa and Dog Island? Is Grandpa still living there secretly? Does Marg know the secret? Is there a Horseshoe Lake connection? Is there a dog chain connection? I've got to find out!

CHAPTER 9

"Yuk! Yuk!"
"This stuff stinks!"
"It's so slimy!"
"Do we have to touch it?" Hilda asked.
"Here are some tools," Sam called. "Grab one and dig into the pot."
"Be careful. It could burn your skin." Mable warned.
Raymond and the crew had finished the end of the canoe and they had turned it upside down on a frame. All of the seams had been stitched with spruce roots and now, it was ready for the final stage. Blobs of the black, stinky goo had to be spread over every seam, inside and outside.
"Watch out!"

"You got that in my hair! Yuk!"

Eventually, every seam was covered with pitch, making a patchwork pattern of black lines across the light brown sheets of bark on the outside and contrasting nicely with the white bark on the inside. This concert of lines, shapes and colour was now left to dry and to harden.

***

School soon drew to a close. Raymond had passed Math. The dogs were coming along nicely with their training. Jack was moping around because Hilda had made up with her boyfriend back home and she would be gone in a week or so. The canoe was ready for its maiden voyage.

"Will it actually float?"

"It looks like a bunch of patches."

"What do you expect? It is a bunch of patches."

"Did people actually use things like this?" Hilda wanted to know.

"Okay, guys. Give me a hand," Sam said as he grabbed one end of the canoe that was sticking out the end of the bus. Sam and Mable had brought the class by bus to the beach to launch their canoe for the first time.

"This is exciting. We're all going to get a chance to try out the canoe."

"I'm not sure I want to get a chance. It looks pretty risky."

"Okay," Sam called. "Who's first? Get your life jackets on. You may need them."

"Here are the paddles," Mable said as she handed them to the students.

Raymond did not want to go first, but just then Hilda grabbed his arm and said, "Come. You show me how to work

Indian transportation." Everyone laughed in fun. They were all having a great time.

The two canoeists put the canoe into the water along the beach. They pushed out a ways in their bare feet and then they stepped into the tipsy canoe and knelt between the thwarts. Hilda took the bow and Raymond, the stern. Raymond didn't exactly know how to steer, but he managed to get the canoe headed into deeper water.

"It floats!"

"Yea!"

"Paddle hard!" someone yelled.

Raymond had to laugh.

"Paddle hard!" he yelled back.

Water was leaking through some of the seams but, amazingly, the canoe stayed afloat and it responded to the motion of the paddles.

What a beautiful day!

Calm blue water lapped at the white sandy beach. Warm sunshine glinted off the water and cast a shadow of the canoe on the soft ripples from the paddles.

If I practiced, I could canoe like Grandpa. When I make my own canoe and paddle to Dog Island, Marg will be proud of me. Maybe Grandpa will be proud of me too, if I find him.

"Indian warrior!" Hilda yelled, as she pointed to Raymond.

"Where is his feather?" someone yelled back.

Everyone laughed.

I like being Indian and I don't need a feather.

Between each use of the canoe, water had to be drained, but, all in all, it worked beautifully. Each student had a chance to try it out.

"Sam and Mable!" the students chanted.

"Sam and Mable!"

At last, Sam and Mable agreed to have a turn. As instructors, they hadn't been sure they could actually pull off this job. They had taken the challenge and this was the reward for being successful. It was a great feeling. They had enjoyed working with these kids and they were happy to share some of their aboriginal culture.

Sam and Mable had failed to notice the scheming going on among the students as they finished their turn in the canoe. Just as they came into shallow water, every student came splashing into the water, kicking and spraying water over the instructors. Finally, the canoe was upset and Sam and Mable were dumped into the water. Everyone was wet, but this was a day to remember. A soggy, but happy bunch, headed for school.

"Hey Raymond, you smell a lot better than the last time we rode this bus," Hilda chided. Everyone laughed.

Too bad that kid is leaving next week. I would still like to be her Indian warrior.

CHAPTER 10

"Help!" Gurgle.
"Help!" Gurgle. Splash.
Why was I so foolish? Some Indian warrior I am!
"Help!" Gurgle. Splash.
Another whitecap caught Raymond in the face as he struggled to hang onto his canoe. Several seams were breaking apart and the canoe was starting to sink.

"Emily!"

I must have lost her. No! No!

How could I have done such a thing? Last winter I nearly killed my brother, Larry, and now my sister, Emily, has drowned. Nooo!

***

Raymond's summer had gone quickly. He had put on more muscles and he had grown even taller. Kohkom had shown him how to braid his hair and he liked it that way. He was proud of his aboriginal heritage. His summer job kept him busy and training the dogs provided a great deal of enjoyment. His father and Marg had given him some birch bark and over the summer, he had constructed his own birch bark canoe. He was proud of it, especially the enlarged stem and headboard. They displayed his original art work. It took a lot of time and energy to piece the bark together, to stitch it with spruce roots and to patch the seams with pitch. He had to fashion his own gunwales, thwarts, sheeting and ribs. It wasn't as nice as the one at school, but it worked.

On a beautiful, fall day, Emily had asked Raymond for a ride in his canoe. He had been out several times already and the canoe handled okay. He had to make a few adjustments while paddling, but, all in all, he was very happy with it. Today would be the perfect day to try it out with two people. Jack helped Raymond to take the canoe to the beach on the back of his old, rust-bucket of a truck.

Everything was in order. Raymond had his backpack. They each had their life jackets on and the water was perfect. How could anything be better? Emily paddled in the front and Raymond, in the stern. The sand dunes soon slipped into the distance, showing the splendor of colour common to Northern Alberta at this time of year. The bright yellow of the birch and poplar trees was interspersed with the bursts of red from the cherry trees and saskatoon bushes. The rolling forms of the Marten Hills capped by Marten Mountain and the undulations of the Sawridge Hills rising before the expanding horizon of Flattop, provided an amphitheatre of sight and sound for the two forms in the birch bark canoe.

However, as is so often the case on days like this, a slight breeze from the east started to blow and the unsuspecting canoeists were lulled into going farther from shore than they had realized. They missed the tell-tale signs of an impending storm.

Such was the case for Raymond and Emily. Brother and sister were having a great time relating stories of happenings from this summer and summers past. Little did they realize how far they were being propelled from shore by the ever increasing east wind. Raymond could see Dog Island looming in the distance and he thought this would be the perfect day to canoe there to check around for signs of Grandpa. Emily wouldn't mind and they wouldn't spend a lot of time there. Just a quick look around and then they would head for home.

Too late, Raymond realized they were being pushed ahead by a strong tail wind. Looking back, he was shocked to see the bulging storm clouds raging in across the sand dunes, sweeping the canoe away from the beach. It was too late to turn around. Their only hope was to get to Dog Island and to wait out the storm.

Raymond's canoe handled the increasing waves smartly and he used his skill to keep from going into the trough of the waves. Emily was a great help, keeping the front of the canoe aligned properly. Up and down they went, all the time heading roughly toward the island. A looming fear started swelling inside Raymond and this gave periodic knots to his guts. He was facing the curse of Dog Island once again. The sun was now blocked by the billowing storm and a hazy glow cast its pall over the greenish-silvery spruce trees on the island. What if the storm swept them past the island? No! That couldn't happen. It would be a hundred kilometres of uncontrolled swirling, twisting and bouncing. Maybe they would drown. Maybe that was what happened to Grandpa. Raymond had flashes of his dream sweep into his mind. His skin boat had swirled and sunk beneath the waves as it filled with water.

"Help! Help!"

"Emily!"

Sputter. Sputter.

"Emily!"

The last Raymond saw of Emily occurred when a huge wave swept over their canoe, swamping it in the resulting trough. Emily had been ejected out of the front of the canoe. When she hit the water, her life jacket came loose and flipped over her head. It must not have been tied properly. Raymond's life jacket was keeping him afloat, but he was desperately trying to search for Emily. Emily could swim, but she could never survive long in these conditions. As he fought to hang onto the overturned canoe, a dark cloud of depression swept over Raymond. The canoe would stay afloat for awhile, but it was now starting to rip apart.

"Help!" Gurgle. Splash.

A mountainous whitecap hit the canoe and Raymond was completely submerged under the tumbling canoe. His hand felt something. He grabbed on and he realized it was Emily. She was hanging onto a thwart of the canoe. Every so often, she could pull herself up into the air pocket trapped beneath the canoe.

She's still alive, but for how long?

"Pole hard!" he thought he had heard someone call.

"Pole hard!" Raymond yelled into the waves.

Raymond had no pole, but once he thought his foot hit something. There it was again. Both feet touched it this time. Another huge wave swept over the tossing craft. As Raymond went into the trough, he realized his feet were touching bottom.

Bottom! Lake bottom.

"Sand bar!" Sputter. Sputter.

This is a sand bar coming out from Dog Island.

"Hang on, Emily! We're going to make it!"

CHAPTER 11

"Hey! Do you need help?" someone yelled from a large, commercial fishing boat.

"Help!" Raymond managed to gasp, between sputters of soggy breath.

"My sister is under here!" Raymond pointed to the gyrating, bark-skinned canoe.

"What are you doing out here? You're lucky we came by with this boat."

"Come up here!" the two men insisted, but Raymond refused.

"Get my sister! I think she has drowned!"

One man grabbed Emily and he started working to revive her. After a time of sputtering and coughing, she seemed to be breathing okay.

"I'm okay!" Emily called to Raymond. "Thanks for the ride. I'm going to go home with these two, good looking guys." Everyone laughed as she was wrapped in a big blanket.

"Come along, son. Get in. You can get that birch bark contraption later. We've got to get to deeper water."

"You go ahead. I'll drag this thing onto the island," Raymond said, in a shivering voice. He was just happy to be alive, to know that he hadn't killed Emily, after all.

"Emily! Tell Mom I decided to stay the night on the island. I'll fix up the canoe and bring it home tomorrow, if it's nice."

"Whatever you say," the man said. "We'll come by later and see how you're doing."

Now the rain started to pour. Not that Raymond could get any wetter, but the rain was cold and it made everything on the island wet and cold. Daylight was fading fast and he knew he would need fire soon to keep from becoming hypothermic. Raymond recalled another time on the island when he was trying to keep his brother Larry from becoming hypothermic. That was in the middle of a blizzard, but, at least, Raymond was dry. Now he was the one needing attention and there was no one else around, or was there?

What are these big boot prints? Are these prints from the fishermen? But they didn't come ashore. Somebody is here and he has big boots. Could this be Grandpa, or someone who knows about Grandpa?

Raymond finished dragging the broken canoe onto the beach. This beach was more rock than sand, and it was littered with driftwood. He was sure the winter camp was on the other side of the island. It would be hard to find good bush camp materials here. Raymond turned the canoe upside down and he draped it over a driftwood log. His backpack was still lashed to a thwart. It had his survival gear inside.

Grandpa's tinder box. Yes! Here it is and it's still dry. I'll have to find some kindling under this pile of driftwood.

Even though it had rained, much of the driftwood was still tinder dry from the hot summer drought and it caught fire, with the help of Raymond's kindling. Soon, a blazing fire was throwing heat to the shivering boy and drying his water-soaked clothes and gear.

It won't be like eating at Kohkom's, but I do have some pemmican and energy bars in my pack. I'll be okay.

The storm passed and an arch of blazing colour, like a kaleidoscope, extended over the western horizon. The red, orange, and yellow streams of light contrasted with the darker blue and black of the storm clouds still heading west over the lake.

Too bad Emily is missing this.

Raymond bunked down under the partially overturned canoe and he basked in the glow of the warm fire.

I hope I have good dreams tonight. At least Larry won't be yelling at me.

***

Morning broke sunny and warm. The sunrise beams struck Raymond in the face and he woke up in good spirits. He revived the fire and put his camp pan over it to make tea. Packaged oatmeal would give a good start to his day.

I'll have to check the island for spruce gum to patch the split in my canoe. I can also check around for signs of the steamship days. Maybe I'll find some signs of Grandpa. Who made those big boot prints, anyway?

After breakfast, Raymond walked along the beach.

I wish there was a map of this place. I think the homestead was on this side of the island, but I can't find any signs of it.

After a long walk, without finding any signs of previous life on the island, Raymond came back to his camp site for a snack.

Whoa! Look at these!

Raymond had discovered more, big boot prints.

Whoever made these prints was a big guy and it looks as if he were checking out my camp. Wow! Look at these paw prints. This was some big dog or a wolf or a combination. Yikes! I'm not sure I want to be stranded on this island.

As he headed for the large spruce trees on the other side of the island to look for spruce pitch, Raymond walked cautiously, always checking behind him to see if he were being followed.

This is getting creepy!

The rocky shore soon gave way to big timber and thick underbrush, some of which hung over the shoreline. Raymond had to choose whether to go into the water or to head into the tall trees. He decided to walk in the water for awhile. At least he could see what was ahead and behind. Just as the overturned canoe slipped out of sight, Raymond heard a whirring sound coming from across the water.

What is that?

As it came closer, Raymond could make out the form of a watercraft.

Is the fishing boat coming back for me?

In a way, Raymond was hoping for a boat. This island was giving him the creeps and it would take a long time to find enough spruce gum to patch his canoe. Even if he did find lots, he didn't have anything to temper it with and there was no guarantee it would hold the bark together until he got back to the mainland.

A seadoo!

I don't believe it. It looks like the redhead and her blond sidekick. Oh, no! Not more trouble!

It was hard to tell, but it looked as if the girls were racing to the far side of the island on a seadoo that had a stream of water spurting out the back end. They soon disappeared in a spray of water.

Raymond decided to get out of the water and to head into the trees. He spent a lot of time crawling over fallen trees, searching out older trees that had large gobs of pitch oozing from old injuries. He gathered up a pocketful and then he decided to turn back toward the canoe.

I've been tramping around for a long time and I haven't seen any sign of a past homestead. That story may just be some more of Marg's legend stuff. Legend or no legend, this is a pretty scary place. I'll just do one more loop.

As Raymond made his last loop through the trees, he heard a dog barking in the distance.

What is that? Is that coming from the giant dog that left those paw prints by my campsite?

Everything was quiet in the trees where Raymond stood, but he could hear screams mixed in with the howling and barking from the other side.

It's coming closer! I'm out of here! Which way to the canoe?

Raymond started running, but the tangle of fallen trees and dead branches made it hard for him to make any progress. The dead branches, with the stringy, old man's beard hanging down, seemed to reach out and snag his shirt. Panting and sweating, he finally reached the clearing. As he stopped to catch his breath, the barking and screaming came crashing into the willows along the edge of the trees.

"Help!"

"Help us!" two girls screamed, as they burst from the willows. A ferocious, snarling animal closed in on the girls. It attacked the legs of the second girl, causing her to fall on the jagged pieces of rock and driftwood.

"Help me!" she screamed, as the attacking dog-wolf, lunged forward with flashing, slashing fangs.

CHAPTER 12

"Help!" the girl screamed. "Help!"

The first girl turned to help, but the enormous beast lunged toward her as well.

"Help!!" the girls screamed. "Help!!"

As Raymond was running to the canoe, he turned toward the screaming, in time to see the dog's attack on the two girls.

Trip!

Snap!

Thunk!

Raymond hit the ground and then he saw that he had tripped over a piece of chain.

"Help!! Help!!" The screams now betrayed a state of complete panic.

After Raymond picked himself up from the ground and saw what was happening, he realized how overpowered the girls were by the dog-wolf. He also realized that he would be a better match for this beast than the girls were.

I have to help, but what can I do? That beast will come for me if I go over there.

Adrenalin started pumping through his body and his muscles tensed from the anger that started boiling within him. It was the same as when he was a warrior, defending his grandpa in his dream. Raymond looked around for a club.

The chain! Where is the chain?

Raymond grabbed for the chain. It was a broken chain that had been wrapped around a post. When he yanked on the chain, a part of the post broke off, giving Raymond a ready made club.

This is a nice club and with a chain on the end, I can swing it around to drive off the dog.

Raymond ran to the attack scene with the club at the ready. As predicted, the big beast charged at Raymond. It knocked him to the ground and lunged for his throat.

The chain! Use the chain!

The post was useless at close range, but Raymond swung the chain at the dog. It looped around his neck. Raymond yanked the post.

"Take that, you ugly canine!" Raymond yelled.

The chain was loose, but solid enough to twist the dog's head away from Raymond's throat.

With all of the rolling, kicking and screaming, it was hard to determine who was winning. Blood spots were showing on the teeth of the beast.

A long, shrill whistle stopped the fight. The whistle came from a big Indian man who was standing in the shadows of the big timber.

The dog immediately high-tailed it to the trees and both man and beast dissolved into the forest.

I don't believe this! How do I get into so much trouble every time I come to Dog Island? It seems like a dream, but the blood on my hand is pretty real.

"Raymond!" someone yelled.

"Raymond!"

It was the redhead. She was half-hysterical, her eyes flashing with fear. The blond girl followed, crying and bleeding from scratches and bites on her arms and legs.

"What are you doing out here?" Raymond asked, as the two girls charged up to him.

"Thanks for fighting off that dog," the redhead said. "Are you okay?"

"Yeah, I think it was half wolf," Raymond said.

"Larry said you were out here and we came to look for you. We've never been here before and we're scared. Larry wouldn't come because he said this place is haunted and he nearly died over here. Our seadoo quit and we can't get it started," the redhead gasped.

"We started walking through the trees to this side of the island and then that ugly monster started chasing us," the blond girl said, through her tears.

"Okay! Okay! Slow down! Come with me. We'll get something to drink and we'll look after our battle scars."

Raymond stirred up the fire and he started heating water for tea. None of the wounds were serious, but tetanus shots would be important to have when they got home. Raymond used things in his first aid kit to patch up the wounds as well as he could for now.

I'm scared too. I wonder who that was and why the dog was attacking us.

The sun was high in the bright, blue sky. The beach was now warm and dry. Warm tea made everyone feel a lot better. They were no longer being chased. The wounds were patched up and they felt more comfortable about talking.

"Your seadoo is stuck?"

"Well, no, not exactly." It was Arlene, the redhead, who replied.

"What do you mean?" Raymond asked.

Raymond realized that, for the first time, he was talking to this girl and he was not worried about the dreadful things she would do or say to him.

"We're not stuck. We just can't get the machine started. It quit when we got into the weeds and now it won't start," the blond girl, Susan, explained.

Raymond had never really looked at these girls before. They often hung around with Larry and they always gave Raymond a rough time. Now, he noticed Arlene's long, red hair and her freckled complexion. Her hazel eyes weren't exactly beautiful, yet they held a mystique that challenged Raymond to find out more. She gave a quick smile.

Smile! No braces!

Susan seemed to be a follower, yet her blond hair and brown eyes set her apart from the redhead. She seemed independent, in her own way.

"Let's find that post and chain," Raymond said. "I'd like to take a closer look at it."

Raymond and the girls found the blood-smeared chain, half buried in the dirt. He looked to see if there was an initial on the end. There it was. The letter "A" was scratched into the chain. Someone had tied dogs to this post a long time ago. Did the "A" stand for Alphonse?

Did Grandpa tie up his dogs here on Dog Island? Is this the other end of the chain I found near Horseshoe Lake? I'm going to take this to Marg's to see if they match.

On the way back to the canoe, Raymond told the girls about his connection to Dog Island, about the disappearance of his Grandpa and the chain.

"Maybe that was your Grandpa and Shadow that chased us," Arlene said.

"No! Shadow was a white, husky dog. He was a sled dog, not a monster wolf-dog that attacked people. My Grandpa wouldn't keep such a dog! Kohkom says he had the best dog team in the country. He was a wise elder."

Back at the canoe, Arlene related a story of her own.

"My kohkom said that she and some friends came over here one time and they found an old Indian burial ground. The rumour was that a medicine man was buried there and when you ran across his grave your hair would stand on end."

"Did it happen?" Susan asked.

"I don't know. Kohkom never said."

"Well, my kohkom said that when she was a little girl, she saw a phantom, white horse swim from the island and disappear onto the mainland," Susan said.

"Well, my kohkom said people used to have tea parties over here during the steamship days," Raymond said.

"Hey, wait a minute!" Raymond gulped.

"You both have kohkoms?"

"Yes," Arlene said. "I am Métis. My kohkom is Indian. I look like a white person so I never wanted to let on that I am an Indian."

"Me too," Susan said. "I'm Métis and my kohkom is Indian. My hair is naturally dark, but I dye it and no one knows I'm an Indian. That's why we look up to you, Raymond."

"Yeah, that's why you're our hero. You're an Indian and you're proud of it, even when people say bad things about you being Indian and stuff," Arlene said.

"Wait just a minute! I'm your hero and you treat me like scum!"

"If you fix our seadoo, we'll be nice to you from now on."

"That sounds like blackmail to me."

"It is."

"Come on! Let's see if we can get your seadoo started."

The seadoo was swamped in a mixture of tall grass, cattails and short willows.

Raymond checked the engine. He cleared out the weeds and he checked the gas.

"Lots of gas."

The battery on the electric starter was dead because they had drained it, trying to start the engine. Raymond tried the pull start, but nothing happened.

"Do you have any tools with this washing machine?" Raymond asked.

They all laughed.

"I'll have you know this is a very expensive washing machine and I'll be in big doodoo if my brother catches me and he finds out I took it to Dog Island," Susan said.

"You stole it from your brother?"

"Well, he's at work and we had to come out to rescue you. Remember? You're our hero!"

"Give me a break!"

Raymond took the spark plug out and dried it off. A few pulls later, the engine started purring nicely.

"Hero! Hero!" the girls chanted. "Great Indian warrior."

"Do you want a ride home?" Arlene asked.

"Well, I won't get my canoe fixed for another day or so and I'm starving for some of my kohkom's cooking. If you give me a ride, I'll see if my kohkom will cook us up some moose meat and bannock. Then, you can see if your kohkum's cooking is as good as my kohkom's."

Everyone laughed.

"Bring that water beater around to the canoe and I'll pick up my things. The fixing will have to wait for another day," Raymond said.

As they were taking the machine around the overhanging trees, a motor boat started coughing and sputtering from around the bend in the shoreline. The big Indian was in the back and his monster dog up front. They were headed for the north shore.

"That engine needs a tune up," Raymond said. "I guess the island was getting too crowded. Whoever he was, he had big feet and a wolf for a dog."

I'm sure that wasn't Grandpa, but maybe that guy had something to do with Grandpa's going missing. What's the connection between the chain at Horseshoe Lake and this one? Why did Grandpa think Horseshoe Lake had bad spirits? Are all of these things connected? Mother won't talk about it and Marg is getting upset with me for asking so many questions. How can I find out what's going on?

Raymond put rocks into the canoe to hold it down. He put out the fire, gathered up his stuff and piled onto the machine with the girls. Susan was up front steering; Arlene was behind her. Raymond slid up, half on and half off the back seat.

"Put your arms around me and hang on," Arlene instructed.

Away they went, headed for the mainland.

Raymond was sad to leave his prized canoe behind, but he knew he could fix it up.

I'LL BE BACK!!

Strands of red hair fluttered across Raymond's face and the spray from the front reflected the sunlight to make a rainbow of colour across the riders.

Raymond hung on a little tighter and a big grin opened up on his face.

I like it! I like it!

"We must look like a wounded whale with water spouting out the wrong end!" Raymond yelled. The girls laughed.

Wow! What a beautiful day in Slave Lake! I've made two new friends, and they think I'm an Indian warrior. I am an Indian warrior!

I think Arlene likes me, and we're headed to Kohkom's for food.

"Food! Yea! I'm starving!"

Life is good!

RETURN TO DOG ISLAND